THE MASK

A novelization by Madeline Dorr
Based on the screenplay by Mike Werb
Story by Michael Fallon
and Mark Verheiden

A PARACHUTE PRESS BOOK

A PARACHUTE PRESS BOOK
Parachute Press, Inc.
156 Fifth Avenue
New York, NY 10010

Photo Credits
Darren Michaels: p.49 (bottom), p.53, p.55 (bottom), p.56 (top).
Rico Torres: p.52.
Kimberly Wright: p.49 (top), p.50, p.54, p.55 (top), p.56 (bottom).
Cover photo by Blake Little.
With special thanks to Fran Lebowitz and Judith Verno.

Printed in the U.S.A.
June 1994
ISBN: 0-938753-80-0
10 9 8 7 6 5 4

PROLOGUE

Long, long ago, the Vikings took to the seas in search of new lands and adventure. The ones who sailed with the great Leif Ericson went on the most dangerous journey of all. They guided their ship through rough, pounding waves, searching for the most forbidding coastline they could find.

"We'll leave it here," Captain Ericson said, pointing out a particularly dark and empty stretch of sand. "So it will never be found."

"Can't we open it just *one* more time?" his first mate asked, looking at the heavily chained and padlocked iron box in the bow of the boat.

The rest of the crew nodded eagerly.

Captain Ericson shook his head. "It's much too dangerous," he said. "We must rid the world of its powers forever."

A gray-haired hag sat next to the box, silently mouthing the chant she was going to use. It always looked silly when she forgot the words in the middle of casting a spell.

Once they were ashore, the men dug a deep hole in front of some rugged rocks and then buried the box inside. They stamped the dirt down and then stepped back.

"Be quick, woman," Ericson said. "We have traveled to the end of the world for this."

The hag nodded. She unrolled a weathered parchment scroll and uncapped a magic powder. As she scattered the powder across the ground, she sneaked a few peeks at her hand, where she'd written notes to help her remember the spell.

"Thy mischief dwell now in waters base and bland," she chanted. "And in waves and sand, thy magic forever sleep."

"She is *so* depressing," one of the crewmen said to another, who nodded.

The hag frowned at them. Then she straightened her robes, and raised her head high. "Lock the box, shut every door," she chanted. "Please don't come back anymore!"

"*Much* better," the crewman said, and his friend nodded again.

Just then, a strong wind kicked up and a black wall of clouds appeared above. The sky exploded in thunder and lightning.

"Whoa," a crewman said. "*Cool.*"

"Back to the ship, men," Ericson commanded. "Hurry!"

"Captain, you've discovered a new world," his first mate said. "It is your right to name it."

Ericson shook his head. "We'll leave that to any poor fools who settle here," he said, and shuddered. "This land is now *cursed*."

Centuries passed, and the winds and waves washed endlessly over the spot where the mysterious box was buried. Gradually the pounding ocean pushed away the dirt and sand that covered the box. Finally, one day, the heavy locks and chains rusted through and the cover burst open. Something exploded out of the box in a cloud of bubbles—and shrieking giggles—and shot toward the surface. Instantly, lightning flashed and thunder roared across the skies of the modern city in the distance.

The Mask was free. Now it could wreak its mischief on an unsuspecting world.

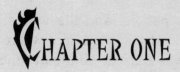CHAPTER ONE

As lightning flashed and thunder cracked through the air, everyone in the Edge City Bank looked outside. A minute ago, the morning sunlight had been pouring through the windows.

"Now, where did *that* come from?" Charlie Schumacher, one of the bank officers, asked. He frowned at his co-worker, who was waiting patiently with a computer printout.

"I wish I could tell you," the bright and friendly young man answered.

"Me too," Charlie said. "So what's up, manly Stanley?"

Stanley Ipkiss forced a smile. "Don't call me that, okay, Charlie?" he asked. He hated being called "manly Stanley." Handing the printout to Charlie, Stanley said, "Let's go over these numbers. We're supposed to have a complete report for the boss before lunch."

Charlie took one look at the complex printouts and tossed them aside. "Be a pal and a half and handle this for me, will you?" he asked. "I'll owe you a large one."

Stanley sighed and took the printouts back. He always ended up doing Charlie's work for him. He never knew how to say no.

Maggie, who was one of the bank's tellers, came walking up. She was cute with curly brown hair, and Stanley had a crush on her. "You needed to see me?" she asked him.

Stanley perked up. "Oh, yes! I did. I mean, I *do*. I got those concert tickets for the show you wanted to see." He reached into his pocket with a magician's flourish and dramatically pulled out two tickets.

"You're kidding!" Maggie said, and examined them happily. "Oh, Stanley, this is great."

"What time should I pick you up?" he asked, running his hand nervously through his mousy brown hair. "I mean, we can eat first, or have a snack after."

Maggie looked troubled. "See, here's the thing," she said. "My *best* girlfriend just got into town, and she's dying to go to this concert. Can we get an extra ticket for her?"

Stanley shook his head. "I had to sell my stereo to get these. There are no more tickets."

"Oh." Maggie sighed. "Well, I can't let her sit home all alone, when she came all this way to see me." Reluctantly, she held out the tickets. "I guess I can't go."

Stanley hesitated. "No, that's okay," he said sadly. "You can go with your friend. I don't like concerts that much anyway. You know, there's all that—music."

"You are so nice," Maggie said. "Really. Charlie, isn't he just the nicest guy?" She gave them a little wave and hurried off to her teller's window, triumphantly holding her tickets.

"That was the most sickening display I've ever witnessed," Charlie said. "I'm nauseated—actually nauseated."

"Wait a minute," Stanley said defensively. "What was I supposed to do?"

"She used the *N* word," Charlie said. "*Nice*. Did you ever hear the saying, 'Nice guys finish last'?"

Stanley frowned. That was pretty much the way it was with him. Stanley was sure that if he looked up the word *nice* in the dictionary, the definition would read: Stanley Ipkiss.

"What you need is a change of pace, buddy," Charlie said. "Tonight I'm going to take you to the hottest new club in town. The CoCo Bongo Club. Only the best people get in."

"So how do *we* get in?" Stanley asked.

"Just leave everything to me," Charlie said, sounding confident. "Tonight is going to be perfect!"

Outside, there was another threatening burst of thunder and lightning. Seconds later, people on the street raised umbrellas and scrambled for cover as a heavy rain began to fall.

Later that day, Charlie stared at the front door of the bank like a retriever spotting its prey.

"Take a look at that," he said to Stanley.

A gorgeous young woman had just come inside. She was holding a soaking wet newspaper over her head to try to protect herself from the rain. The woman had long blond hair and ice-blue eyes.

"Excuse me," she said. "Where can I open a new account?"

Charlie flashed his best hundred-watt smile. "Right here," he said, stepping in front of Stanley. "Take a seat."

The woman nodded, but sat down at Stanley's desk. Charlie was stunned by his near miss—his smile always worked—and Stanley was stunned by his good luck. Flustered, he hurried behind his desk and missed his chair, crashing to the floor. Blushing furiously, he sprang back up and sat down.

"So, uh, what kind of bank account did you have in mind?" he asked in his most businesslike voice.

The woman smiled sweetly. "Well, I'm not exactly sure. I'm terrible with things like that, Mr.—?"

Stanley blinked and checked the nameplate on

his desk. "Ipkiss," he said. "Stanley Ipkiss."

The woman extended a delicate hand. "Tina Carlyle," she said. "Pleased to meet you."

Stanley shook her hand awkwardly. "The, uh, pleasure's all mine."

Tina took a small makeup mirror from her shoulder bag and daintily blotted some raindrops from her face as Stanley watched. When she saw Stanley staring, she snapped the mirror closed and said, "What an interesting tie you have, Mr. Ipkiss."

Stanley looked down. "Oh. It's a power tie, you know? They're supposed to make you feel" —he smiled uncertainly—"powerful."

"Does it work?" Tina asked very sweetly.

Since it didn't, Stanley frowned. "Well—it's just a tie." He coughed a few times. "Now, about that account," he said, and stuck his pen in the electric pencil sharpener. There was an ugly noise and he pulled out a mangled pen. He stared at the pen and looked flustered again.

Taking advantage of Stanley's embarrassment, Tina went into action. She dropped her mirror in her bag and flicked on a tiny red light attached to the shoulder strap. This activated the small video camera neatly hidden inside. She carefully adjusted the bag, pointing it at the open bank vault a few feet from Stanley's desk, and began taping.

"We have various plans," Stanley said, giving Tina the standard sales pitch.

Tina smiled at Stanley without really listening to him. She was busy taking pictures of the bank vault, the bank guards, the alarm system. But Stanley was concentrating too hard on what he had to say next to spot the secret video camera. He'd never had such a pretty customer before.

"We have savings," Stanley said. "We have checking. Savings and checking. CDs. Savings and CDs. T-bills..."

Tina was casing the bank for a robbery—and Stanley hadn't even noticed!

CHAPTER TWO

Over at the CoCo Bongo Club, there was a serious meeting going on in Dorian Tyrel's office. Dorian was the owner of the club and a very slick gangster. He liked to wear bold, hip suits and never went anywhere without a big diamond stud in his ear.

Tina had returned with the video from the bank, and now Dorian and his sidekick, Dr. Freeze, were watching it. In the back of the office, two other members of the gang, Sweet Eddy and Orlando, were busy playing air hockey.

"Hey, keep it down back there!" Dorian ordered as he sipped nervously on a chocolate soda.

Sweet Eddy and Orlando grumbled, but started playing more quietly.

Dr. Freeze scribbled notes as he watched the video screen. He was tall and thin, with a perfectly sculpted haircut. "That's cool, man," he said. "Freeze it right there."

Dorian punched the pause button. "What do you think, Doctor?" he asked.

"Layout's not bad," Dr. Freeze said with a shrug. "We got us a sweet little Perkins/Janning time lock on the vault. But the security cameras are putting the chill on my thrill."

Dorian looked worried. "Can you pull it off?"

"Hey, man, you're talking to the Doctor here," Dr. Freeze said, sounding insulted. "But what's Niko got to say about this?"

"Nothing," Dorian said, sounding more confident than he felt. "This isn't any of his business."

"Get real, man," Dr. Freeze said. "*Everything* is Niko's business. He owns you, he owns me—he owns this whole town!"

Deep down Dorian knew Dr. Freeze was right. Niko was the "big boss" in Edge City. And Dorian owed him money. A lot of money. The nightclub wasn't doing well, and Dorian had to get fast cash from somewhere. That's why he had come up with the plan to rob the bank.

"Well, I'm about to give Niko a little wake-up call," Dorian said, acting tough. "First we take the bank and then we take Niko." He put on a slow grin. "And then this city is our playground."

As Dorian and his gang plotted, something strange was drifting down the river that ran through the city. It was the mask. Finally freed after centuries in a rusted box, the mask was floating in a nest of seaweed and garbage. Now it washed up onshore under a bridge, where a large rat lived in a hole in the bricks. The rat crept out and sniffed curiously at the mask's time-worn wooden surface. Carefully, the rat took a small nibble.

Instantly, the mask began to shimmer with a strange glow. Then it started vibrating with its own magical inner life. The rat squeaked and jumped back, pushing the mask back into the water. It floated farther downstream, riding the slow-moving current straight into the dark heart of the city.

Outside the bank after work, Charlie leaned out his taxicab window. "Don't forget!" he yelled to Stanley. "Ten o'clock at the CoCo Bongo! You'll love it!"

Stanley wasn't so sure, but he nodded and waved as the cab screeched away.

Stanley went into Ripley's Auto Finishing Shop, where his car was being repaired. The cluttered garage was deserted, and he rang the little service bell sitting on the front counter.

"Hello?" he called, his voice echoing through the shop.

Burt, the owner of the place, lumbered out from the back. Stanley knew instantly that he would never be friends with this unshaven man whose hair looked like it was slicked back with car grease. "Hang on, hang on," Burt grumbled.

Irv, a skinny version of Burt who wore Coke-bottle glasses, popped up from beneath a car. He ripped off a chunk of motor and wiring and held it out. "Hey, Burt," he said. "What's this?"

"Oh, I don't know," Burt said, chuckling. "About seven hundred bucks!"

They both laughed wickedly, and Burt made his way over to Stanley.

"What can I do for you, bub?" he asked, wiping his grease-stained hands across the front of his shirt.

"I'm here to pick up my car. It's the Civic," Stanley answered.

Burt frowned and scratched his head. "Was it kind of a puke-green?"

"Well, actually, they call it emerald forest," Stanley corrected him. "I brought it in for an oil change. I got that discount coupon in the mail. You get a—"

"Irv!" Burt barked, interrupting him. "Puke-green Civic!"

Irv popped back out from beneath the car hood. "*You're* the Civic?" he asked Stanley, a look of pain crossing his face.

"Is it ready?" Stanley asked.

Irv shook his head. "The brake drums are shot and you need a new transmission."

Stanley's eyes widened. "What?!" he cried. "All I wanted was an oil change!"

"Well, you're lucky we caught these other

things in time," Burt said, shrugging.

"I wouldn't put my worst enemy in that car," Irv agreed.

"It's up to you," Burt said. "Fix it or get buried in it." He pulled a grease-marked black plastic comb out of his shirt pocket. "Here's your free comb that comes with the coupon."

Stanley looked at the battered, obviously secondhand comb. "Well, fix the car, of course," he said slowly. "I—"

Burt handed him a blunt pencil. "Okay. Sign here. Press down hard..."

Stanley looked at the worksheet, trying to find the estimate for how much the repairs would cost. "How can I sign it if I don't know what it's going to cost? There's no price," he said uneasily.

Burt chuckled again. "There *will* be."

That sounded expensive, but Stanley had no choice. He signed the paper. "Um, your coupon says that if you keep the car more than twenty-four hours, you will supply a loaner vehicle," he said, giving back the pencil.

"Sure," Burt said heartily. "Irv, bring around the *loaner*."

Irv laughed and disappeared into the back of the shop.

A few minutes later Stanley heard the cough and sputter of an engine. Irv drove up in a rusty, broken-down 1956 Studebaker.

Burt turned back to Stanley, showing all his

teeth in a mean smile. "That'll be nineteen bucks a day," he said, extending his greasy hand for the money.

Stanley started to argue, but then just reached for his wallet. All he'd wanted was an *oil change*.

So far, it just wasn't his day.

CHAPTER THREE

That night, the CoCo Bongo Club was the hottest place in town. Two muscle-bound bouncers stood in front of the doors to the club. Their job was to pick which of the young, well-dressed people crowded outside would be allowed to enter. All the guests were shouting and leaping up and down, hoping to be among the chosen few.

The parking lot was filled with swanky cars. There was a glistening Rolls-Royce, a long white limousine, and a beautiful black Jaguar. As each fancy car drove up to the front of the club, a parking attendant hurried to open the door and park the car.

Then, a rusty old car that looked like it belonged in the junkyard rumbled up to the club. Stanley sat behind the wheel. He wasn't happy. The car door was almost rusted shut, but he finally forced it open with his shoulder and nearly tumbled out into the street.

As he scanned the crowd looking for Charlie, who was supposed to meet him there, he saw a high-class couple frowning at the eyesore-mobile.

"It's a classic," he said, smiling nervously and patting the hood. "Worth a fortune."

The couple sniffed and looked away.

The engine had died. Behind him, the carhops pushed the car down the street with a lot of loud clanking.

"Hey, Stanley," Charlie shouted from the mass of people. "Nice wheels."

Stanley shrugged self-consciously. Then he noticed the life-size poster of Tina Carlyle above the main entrance. It read: FEATURING THE MUSICAL STYLINGS OF MISS TINA CAR-LYLE.

"Hey," he said. "That's the woman from the bank!"

Charlie nodded. "Yeah. Now follow me." He pushed his way through the crush of bodies and then called out to one of the bouncers guarding the door. "Hey, Bobby! What's happening, man?"

Bobby completely ignored him as he ushered a pale rock star dressed in black and his date past the velvet rope barrier and inside.

"Yo, Nick!" Charlie yelled at the other bouncer. "Nicky baby. It's me, Charlie!"

Nick didn't even glance in his direction.

Charlie turned to Stanley. "How much cash you carrying?" he asked.

Stanley checked his wallet. "I don't know. Fifty, sixty bucks."

Charlie motioned for him to hand it over.

"No way," Stanley said.

"You want to stand out here all night?" Charlie asked.

Stanley checked out Tina's poster again, and started counting out some cash.

Charlie snatched the whole wad of money, fanning it out. "Hey, Bobby!"

Instantly, the bouncer came over.

"Charlie, how you doing, man?" the bouncer said. He pocketed the money and unlatched the velvet rope barrier. "Long time no see."

The crowd surged forward and Stanley was knocked aside. He shoved his way to the front just as the rope was latched shut. He fell over it, and the bouncers lifted him up, placing him back outside of it.

"Hey, wait a minute," Stanley protested. "I'm with him! Charlie, wait up!"

But Charlie had already been whisked inside the CoCo Bongo, leaving Stanley out in the rain alone. The bouncers were looking the other way, so Stanley unlatched the rope himself.

The two bouncers grabbed him before he could take a step.

"Never touch the rope," Bobby scolded, and started dragging him through the crowd with Nick's help.

"Careful," Stanley warned. "I bruise easily!"

The bouncers tossed him into the rainy street and returned to their posts.

As Stanley smoothed out his rumpled clothing, a horn blared and a limousine swung into the street. Stanley scrambled out of the way, but was splattered with muddy water. He wiped the dirt out of his eyes just in time to see Tina Carlyle being escorted out of the limo by an umbrella-carrying chauffeur. She was wearing an expensive-looking red dress trimmed with red lace. She looked even more beautiful than the last time Stanley had seen her.

Recognizing him, Tina paused. "Oh—Mr. Ipkiss. Hi."

Stanley knew he looked ridiculous, but he managed a pathetic wave, almost slipping and falling again.

Before Stanley could say anything else, there was a squeal of grinding brakes behind him. It was the carhop pulling up in Stanley's battered loaner. Tina stared at the old heap.

"It's just a loaner," Stanley explained. "My car's in the shop. It's being prepared for...the big race."

Tina looked blank. "What race?"

Stanley thought quickly. "The, uh, Tallahassee 3000. I've won it four years in a row. Consecutively!"

"Wow. That's great," Tina said, impressed.

Stanley nodded. "I've been on fire eight times," he bragged as if it were no big deal. "You get used to it."

"Well, good luck in the race. See you later," she said.

Stanley watched as the crowd parted for her and the bouncers ushered her inside. He got into his jalopy. He drove aimlessly around the streets of Edge City for a while. He was just crossing the Tahoochie Bridge when the car engine started spluttering and then died. He tried over and over, but the car wouldn't start again.

He shoved the rusty door open and got out. Angrily, he kicked the bumper—which fell off with a loud clunk. Then he watched in shock as the front axle collapsed, the tires fell off, and the driver's door clattered to the ground.

Stanley stared at the pile of useless steaming metal. He was stuck in the middle of nowhere, with nothing but the pieces of what used to be a car. What a terrible day.

Suddenly, something caught his eye down in the dark water swirling below the bridge. There, floating along in the river, Stanley saw—a body!

CHAPTER FOUR

Stanley stared at the water. He had to act fast. Someone was in trouble down there!

"Hey!" he yelled. "Hey, mister!"

He rushed down the slippery embankment toward the river, slipping and sliding. A black cat raced past him. Being superstitious, Stanley jumped out of the way only to land on an old mirror, shattering it. Off balance, he ducked underneath an old ladder—his third piece of bad luck in the past few seconds—and splashed into the water.

The water was over his head, but he grabbed at the body, which promptly fell to pieces. The "body" was nothing but a trash bag, an old tire, and some floating garbage—and an old wooden mask.

"Some lifesaver I am," Stanley grumbled.

He climbed out of the water and inspected the mask. Its face looked like a cross between a mischievous clown and an evil witch. It had eerie, diamond-shaped eyeholes with raised wooden eyebrows and a pointy, crooked nose. Its mouth stretched out into a leering grin that seemed to be mocking him. Mysterious curly markings were carved all over the mask. The markings looked like some sort of secret code. As Stanley brought the mask closer to his face, its surface began to shimmer.

Just then, a blinding spotlight beamed down on him.

"Hey, you!" a loud voice boomed.

Stanley looked up and saw a police car.

"What are you doing down there?" shouted a police officer.

Stanley squinted into the light, trying to think of a reasonable answer. "I was looking for"—he held up his waterlogged souvenir—"my mask," he finished weakly. Then he climbed up the riverbank to the police car.

Since Stanley's car had broken apart, the police gave him a ride home.

"Thanks," he said wearily as he dragged himself out and stepped onto the sidewalk.

The cops waved, and as the car pulled away, Stanley was splashed with mud. Again. He sighed and headed for his apartment building. He was very, very tired.

Just as he got to the front steps, a tough-looking guy hopped down from a fire escape. Stanley recognized him. He was in a gang called the Death's Heads. Stanley usually tried to avoid them.

"Hey, you a cop or something?" the guy said.

Six other Death's Head members suddenly appeared out of the shadows, surrounding Stanley.

"I'm not a cop," Stanley said, backing up. "They just gave me a ride home that's all. I haven't got any money. I haven't got a car. All I've got is this, and you're welcome to it." He tossed the gang leader the mask.

The guy scowled at the weird antique, which was still slick with river slime, and threw it back.

"You got us all wrong," he sneered. "We don't want any trouble. I just want the time. You got the time?"

As Stanley pulled his sleeve back to check his watch, the gang's leader pulled out a knife, slicing through the watchband.

"See, I only wanted the time!" he yelled, grabbing the watch and holding up his prize.

The gang members all laughed and began shoving Stanley back and forth. Finally he broke free and ran up his front steps. He fumbled for his keys and opened the door, slamming it behind him. All the while, the punks outside roared with laughter.

Stanley took a deep breath and tiptoed down the hall, his wet shoes squeaking. The people in his building were light sleepers, especially the person who lived in Apartment A. As he passed that door, it flew open. The apartment manager, Mrs. Peenman, appeared, looking like an old dragon. Her hair was in curlers and her black nightgown trailed along behind her like a tail.

"Ipkiss!" she shouted. "Do you have any idea what time it is?"

Stanley looked at his empty wrist. "Actually— no."

"It's three o'clock in the morning!" she screamed. "First you wake up the entire building laughing it up with your pals. Then you—" She stopped, seeing the puddles on the floor. "Look at my new carpet!"

Stanley sighed. "Mrs. Peenman, why don't you go back to monster land with all the other dragons?" he asked under his breath.

"What?" she asked, furious.

"Nothing," he said. "I'm sorry. I think I'll just go to bed now."

He shuffled into his apartment, which was small but neat. It was full of books, and a few pictures of his favorite old cartoons were framed on one wall. Stanley loved cartoons.

Milo, his little terrier, came out from the bedroom. The dog was so happy to see him that he started gagging and coughing.

"Take it easy, Milo," Stanley said, and patted him on the back. "You know you cough when you get too excited. Do you need your asthma spray?"

26

Milo just looked up and wagged his tail.

Stanley headed for his bedroom, where he stored his Looney Tunes collection. He chose one of his favorite cartoons and popped it into his VCR. He quickly changed into his favorite purple paisley pajamas and sat down on his bed to watch the tape.

Milo ran in, yipping and carrying a Frisbee in his mouth.

"Okay, okay," Stanley said, not taking his eyes off the TV screen. "One throw."

He tossed the Frisbee out into the hallway and Milo made a perfect leaping catch. He barked and brought it back.

"Wait," Stanley said, pointing at the television. "This is the best part."

They both watched the cartoon. Stanley laughed loudly and Milo barked excitedly at the screen. Then there was a pounding on the wall. It was coming from Apartment A, right next door.

"Sorry, Mrs. Peenman!" Stanley called out, and ejected the tape. He turned on the TV and switched it to the Larry King talk show. Dr. Arthur Neuman was the guest and he was taking phone calls from around the country.

"That is correct," Dr. Neuman was telling a caller. "We all wear masks. They hide our worst thoughts. They help us trick people into thinking we're happy."

"You don't know the half of it, pal," Stanley

told him. Then he turned off the television and looked at Milo. "I met a woman today, Milo. A singer. She wanted to take me to Hawaii—you know, her treat. But I said I couldn't go because I was too busy being miserable at the bank. Broke her heart." He paused to button up his pajamas. "She was beautiful, though."

Milo sniffed warily at the mask on the bedside table. Then he whimpered and hopped off the bed.

Stanley wandered over and picked up the mask, gently running his fingers across the worn wood. As he did so, he could almost see a strange glow. He could hear drums pounding. It sounded as if haunting, whispery voices were calling his name. Stanley turned toward the mirror and slowly raised the mask to put it on.

Instantly, the mask shrink-wrapped across his face. Then it popped off with a sharp sucking sound.

"Whoa," Stanley said uneasily as Milo whimpered again.

He studied the mask, and then his own face in the mirror. The mask had *seemed* to mold to his face. He *thought* he had heard voices and drums. It must have been his imagination. It was only a dumb old mask, right?

He pressed the mask more firmly to his face and an incredible transformation began. Rubbery wooden whips shot out of the mask and began to wrap around his head. Stanley grabbed his face, trying to take off the mask, but his body started to spin uncontrollably. He spun faster and faster, like a human tornado.

"Helllpppp mmmeeee!" Stanley shrieked. His voice grew higher and higher as he twirled even faster.

Finally, a large hand reached out of the human twister and locked onto the bedpost. The whirlwind screeched to a halt, causing sparks and smoke to rise from the carpet. As the smoke slowly cleared, Milo began yipping wildly at what he saw. Stanley Ipkiss was gone. In his place was a creature named *The Mask!*

CHAPTER FIVE

The Mask was wearing a shiny purple suit. The material had huge curlicues all over it and looked like a bold, jazzy version of Stanley's paisley pajamas. His head was no longer Stanley's head. It was large, bald, and bright green! The enormous bug eyes glowed with mischief and the nose was bony and beaked. The creature's mouth and teeth were enormous and sparkling white as he broke into a huge grin. The whole effect was devilishly loony—but also downright charming.

The Mask checked himself out in the mirror. He liked what he saw.

"S-s-snazzy!" he shouted, and snapped his bow tie with a crazy gleam in his eyes. "It's party time! P-A-R-T-Y! Why? Because I gotta!"

With that, he was off!

The Mask left his apartment and tiptoed down the hall with exaggerated care. Suddenly, a ringing alarm clock leapt out of his suit pocket and started skittering down the hall. He grabbed for it, but missed. So he pulled a huge sledgehammer from the same pocket and pounded at the carpet, smashing craters the size of manhole covers in the floor.

The door of Apartment A burst open and Mrs. Peenman's angry face appeared. When she saw the Mask holding his oversize carnival mallet, she screamed hysterically.

The Mask screamed back, his eyes bulging out on stalks and his mouth expanding to the size of a tuba.

"Easy, lady!" he shouted. "I was just killing time!" Then he shrieked with laughter, literally bouncing off the walls and floor.

Mrs. Peenman grabbed an enormous shotgun and let loose with both barrels. *Ka-boom! Ka-boom!*

The Mask zigzagged back and forth off the walls and leapt straight out the window—plunging swiftly toward the ground seven stories below. He landed with a loud *Splat!* and lay face-down in the middle of the street, as flat as a pancake.

Then he grabbed his head with one arm and peeled himself up off the cement. There was a *Crack!* and he returned to his normal shape.

"Yeow!" the Mask said, his voice sounding like a much rowdier version of Stanley's. "That first step is a *doozy*."

"Hey, mister," the Death's Head gang leader

called from behind some trash cans. "You got the time?"

The Mask turned to see that the gang was all around him—and freaked out by the sight of his green face.

"As a matter of fact, I do!" the Mask said happily, and yanked out a huge pocket watch. "Why, it's just two seconds before I honk your nose!" He held up his long fingers and counted "One, two—" He grabbed the punk's nose, and twisted it hard. "Honk! Honk!" Then the Mask zipped off down the street.

"Ow!" the guy yelped. "Get him!"

But the gang members froze in their tracks. Unbelievably, the Mask was morphing into something else before their very eyes. He was now—a carnival barker! Multicolored lights and happy music came out of nowhere. Then long pink and blue balloons appeared in the Mask's hand. He went into a frenzy, twisting the balloons into different shapes as the gang stared with their mouths hanging open.

"Voila!" the Mask said. "A giraffe for you!" He handed it to the biggest, dumbest gang member and went into another wild flurry of motion. "Why, it's a French poodle!" he said, holding up his creation. "And finally"—he twisted furiously—"my favorite...a machine gun!"

The balloon gun morphed into a *real* gun, and the Mask sprayed the area with hot lead. The punks dove for cover and the Mask tossed the gun aside, thrilled with his newfound powers.

"This is *incredible!*" he raved. "Why, with these powers, I could be a superhero! I could fight crime, work for world peace..." He wiggled his bright bushy eyebrows impishly. "But first, a visit!"

And again the Mask was off!

Over at Ripley's Auto Finishing Shop, Burt and Irv were making a late night of it. They were chowing down chili dogs and sleepily playing cards, when the front door exploded inward.

The Mask leapt inside. "Hello, boys," he said.

"We're closed," Burt grumbled. "Nobody's here."

"*You're* here," the Mask said, showing his gleaming teeth in a big grin. "And I'm here to help you!" He whirled about and yanked two glistening mufflers from the wall. "We'd better do a few touch-ups before you two have some serious trouble!"

He twirled around like a tornado, grabbing tools and hood ornaments and metallic paints. "Let's redecorate!" he yelled cheerfully.

His eyes popped out of his head for a startling rubbery second, and he set himself to whirling work.

Having super powers was fun!

* * * * *

In the morning, Stanley had trouble waking up. At first he wasn't sure where he was, until he saw Milo at the foot of his own lumpy bed. But why did he feel so *strange?*

Then Stanley remembered what he had done last night. He leapt out of bed to look in the mirror. His normal face looked back at him, and he was wearing his same old paisley pajamas. He saw the wooden mask sitting on his dresser. It looked harmless, too.

"It was only a dream," he said, relieved. "Boy, I have to lay off those cartoons."

Just as he was starting to relax, there was a knock on the door. Stanley opened it to find a police officer with gray hair and a wrinkled, hound-dog face.

"Ipkiss?" the cop asked, looking him up and down. "Stanley Ipkiss?"

Stanley gulped and nodded.

The cop flashed a badge. "Lieutenant Kellaway, City Precinct," he said. "You know anything about the disturbance last night?"

Stanley looked blank. "Disturbance, sir?"

Lieutenant Kellaway nodded. "A prowler broke in and attacked Mrs. Peenman."

Stanley swallowed hard. "Attacked her?"

"You didn't hear it?" Lieutenant Kellaway asked suspiciously. "Do you sleep with your head in a hair dryer?" He swung the door open wider to give Stanley a view of the mess in the hall.

Stanley was flabbergasted to see the shotgun blasts in the walls, the potholes left from the gigantic mallet, and the shattered remains of the wacky alarm clock.

Last night hadn't been a dream after all!

CHAPTER SIX

Even when he looked again, Stanley couldn't believe how much damage there was.

"It's—impossible," he gasped.

"No," Lieutenant Kellaway said, staring at Stanley's ugly purple paisley pajamas. "Your *pajamas* are impossible. *This* actually happened. Didn't you hear it?"

Stanley thought quickly. "See, I have this inner ear problem," he explained. "I once slept through an entire Metallica concert."

"Is that a fact?" Lieutenant Kellaway asked, narrowing his eyes.

Stanley held one hand to his ear, pretending to be hard of hearing. "Eh? What's that?"

"Forget it," Lieutenant Kellaway said, and handed him a card. "If you remember anything unusual about last night, I want you to call me."

"Absolutely," Stanley promised. "And good luck in all of your future cases." He closed the door and glanced at the clock on the wall. "Oh, no, I'm late!" He turned and raced into his bed-room to get ready for work.

Out in the hall, Lieutenant Kellaway was now writing down a description of the prowler from Mrs. Peenman.

"Okay," he said patiently. "A green head the size of a pumpkin, purple bodysuit, and shiny shoes." He sighed. "Come on, give me a break, lady."

"I saw what I saw," Mrs. Peenman insisted.

Another police officer ran up the stairs.

"Lieutenant, we just got an emergency call from an auto-body shop on 67th," he said, out of breath. "You're not going to believe the descrip-tion we got on the guy who broke in."

Lieutenant Kellaway glanced at Mrs. Peenman, who was still insisting that she saw what she saw. "Try me," he said dryly.

Inside his apartment, Stanley rushed around, searching for his keys.

"Milo!" he said, tying his tie as he searched. "Keys!"

His dog was great at finding keys. Milo's ears pricked up. He located them under a couch cush-ion, emerging just as Stanley came out with his briefcase.

"Good boy," Stanley said, and patted him.

Before Stanley left, he took one last look at the mask. Its eerie black eyeholes and devilish grin seemed to be mocking him. On a sudden impulse, he grabbed it and threw it out the window with a sigh of relief.

But he didn't see the mask hit a sudden wind gust and boomerang back toward the building. It landed with a thud on the fire escape, its mocking grin glowing with triumph.

For the Mask, the fun had only just begun.

Across town, Ripley's Auto Finishing Shop looked like something out of a wild cartoon. Everything had been painted with polka dots, checks, and plaids. Reporters and curious bystanders had gathered to watch as paramedics wheeled Burt and Irv out of the building on hospital stretchers.

The two men looked as if they belonged in a cartoon too. Their entire bodies were spray-painted bright colors, and hood ornaments were glued to their foreheads.

Lieutenant Kellaway got out of his patrol car to meet the responding officer.

"We were able to get a description, sir," he said, "but it's pretty weird."

Lieutenant Kellaway nodded. "Big green head? Purple suit?"

The cop stared at him. "How did you know, sir?" he asked.

"Lucky guess," Lieutenant Kellaway said.

Just then, a young woman wearing a blazer and blue jeans interrupted the police officers.

"Excuse me, I'm Peggy Brandt with the *Evening Star,*" she said, whipping out her reporter's notepad. "Can you tell me what happened here?"

"No," Lieutenant Kellaway growled. "And you can quote me on that."

As he and the other officers shoved past her, Peggy frowned. Then she slipped underneath the yellow police tape and went inside the garage. Ignoring the wacky cartoon paint job, she sifted through the papers scattered on the floor. One of the repair bills caught her attention and she examined it more closely.

The signature at the bottom read *Stanley Ipkiss.* She decided to track him down. It was the only clue she had.

Across town, Stanley had just hurried into the bank, looking rumpled and unshaven.

"What happened to you last night?" Charlie asked.

"You mean after you left me outside?" Stanley said.

Charlie looked guilty for about one second. "Sorry about that." He held out his newspaper. "But look. Your girlfriend got a nice review."

The *Evening Star*'s entertainment section had a close-up of Tina singing, with the headline "Bombshell Explodes at the CoCo Bongo."

"Boy, is she great," Stanley said longingly.

"Forget her," Charlie advised. "She's not the

kind to be interested in a nice guy like you."

"She happens to be very nice herself," Stanley defended her.

Charlie shook his head. "You need a woman you can depend on. Someone down-to-earth, someone—" He stopped, seeing Peggy Brandt by a teller's window. "Someone like her! Except—I saw her first."

Peggy walked over to them. "Stanley Ipkiss?" she asked.

Charlie reluctantly pointed at Stanley.

"Hi," she said, holding out her hand. "I'm Peggy Brandt, with the *Evening Star*."

Stanley looked guilty. "I had to cancel my subscription," he said. "The paper kept getting stolen and—"

"Actually, I just want to ask you a few questions," Peggy interrupted him. "About Ripley Auto Finishing."

"I, uh, I don't even have a car," Stanley said quickly. "You know, because they pollute, and—"

Peggy whipped out the bill she'd stolen from the auto-body shop. "You don't own a 1989 Civic?"

"Oh, *that* car," Stanley said, and clapped a hand to his forehead. "Yeah, it's all coming back to me. In fact, I may have been in the place once or twice, Miss—" He stopped. "Wait, are you Peggy Brandt, of 'Ask Peggy'?"

She flushed, but nodded.

"Wow," Stanley said, his face brightening. "You printed my letter last year, remember? 'Nice Guys Finish Last.'"

"*You're* Mr. Nice Guy?" Peggy said. "Stanley, do you know how much mail we got from that column? There are *hundreds* of women out there looking for a man just like you."

Stanley looked pleased. "Really?"

"Yes," Peggy said enthusiastically. "It was one of my best pieces ever. But I'm trying to get a job as a real reporter now. It pays better, and I need the money." She moved closer to him. "Stanley, did you ever see or hear anything suspicious at Ripley Auto? Anything at all?"

"No," Stanley said, his face expressionless. "Sorry."

"Oh," Peggy said, clearly disappointed. "Well, if you think of anything, here's my number. My *home* number," she added as she turned to leave.

"You really think there are women out there looking for a guy like *me?*" he asked her eagerly.

"Sure," Peggy said. "And I'm one of them."

With that, she walked out of the bank.

"Wow," Stanley said, and looked down at the phone number she had given him. "How about that..."

CHAPTER SEVEN

Over at the CoCo Bongo Club, the phone rang in Dorian's office. He answered it to find his boss, Niko, on the other end of the line.

"You know what I hate?" Niko said without any other greeting. He was a large, powerful man and was busy lifting weights as he spoke over a wireless headset.

"Wind chimes?" Dorian guessed.

"Besides that," Niko said. "Losing. I hate losing." He dropped his barbells with a clank. "So why is your club losing my money?"

"It takes time to make a club swing," Dorian said defensively. "It'll be a gold mine by spring." Dorian smiled knowingly to himself. He had a plan. A plan to get money. A plan to rob the Edge City Bank.

"Make it work now," Niko said, "or pick out the suit."

"What suit?" Dorian asked.

"The one you're going to be buried in," Niko

answered, and abruptly hung up.

That night, Stanley had trouble sleeping. He tossed and turned for hours. He was about to get a glass of milk when he saw the mask grinning at him through the window—seven floors above the ground. Stanley stood, frozen, staring at the moonlit face. Once again he thought he heard the same faint voices calling his name and the sound of pounding drums.

"No," he said weakly, backing away from the window.

Yet he could not resist the possibilities of what he could do with the mask. He climbed out onto the narrow ledge in his pajamas.

"Just one last time," he whispered, and reached out for the glowing mask.

His foot slipped. As he fell, he screamed and jammed the mask to his face. Instantly, he was whirled back up. The apartment window shattered inward as the Stanley Mask tornado burst into the room. Milo cringed and hid under the bed.

The tornado scorched the rug as it wheeled around the room and slammed to a stop, revealing the Mask in his full glory.

"I gotta be me!" he sang with his arms held high. He zipped into the bathroom and stuck the newspaper picture of Tina on the bathroom mirror. Then he started madly brushing his teeth, spraying on cologne, and batting himself with a powder puff—all at the same time. He whipped a big banana-yellow hat out of nowhere, cocked it on his head, and paused to admire himself.

"S-s-smokin'!" he said cheerfully. Then he searched his pockets frantically. "Can't make the scene without the green. No dough, no show!"

He zipped energetically away to go find some money.

The Mask wasn't the only one looking for money. Parked in the empty street in front of the Edge City Bank was a van full of Dorian's men. They were planning a robbery to improve their cash flow.

"Let's go," Dr. Freeze said. "The Doctor is ready to operate!" He turned to the others. "No mistakes, boys."

Suddenly, an alarm started ringing.

"Who did that?" Dr. Freeze demanded. The others shrugged innocently.

Before the burglars could pick the bank's lock, the glass front doors crashed open and a whirling figure shot outside. It zigzagged down the street, leaving a flurry of twenty-dollar bills drifting down onto the stunned robbers.

Then the whirlwind did a U-turn and raced back.

It was the Mask! He was carrying huge sacks of money. "Would you guys hold my money?" He handed each of the openmouthed crooks a sack. Before they could react, he playfully slapped each of their faces. Then he grabbed the sacks back and zoomed off, wild laughter trailing behind him.

"After him!" Dr. Freeze ordered.

The robbers ran back to the van and roared away in hot pursuit. As they did, two police cars zoomed around the corner with their sirens blaring and joined the chase.

The Mask laughed even louder and picked up speed. He was heading to the hottest spot in town, and no one could catch him.

Outside the CoCo Bongo Club, the usual crowd of people trying to look cool enough to get inside were waiting. A buzz of excitement traveled through the group as they saw the longest limousine in the world pull up by the entrance.

The door opened and the Mask stepped out grandly.

"Ah," he said with a wave. "My public!"

Bobby the bouncer actually looked a little shaky as the Mask sashayed up to him.

"Are you, uh, on the list?" Bobby asked.

"No," the Mask said. "But I believe my friends Lincoln, Jackson, and Franklin are. Here, look—" He whipped out a wad of bills and pointed out the pictures on the fives, the twenties, and the hundreds.

Then he tossed the cash in the air and strutted

into the club.

The CoCo Bongo Club was almost as wild as the Mask himself with its colorful tropical decorations. There were exotic birds perched in huge, sprawling trees, a working waterfall with a pool and palm tree island, and a crowded dance floor.

The Mask was seated at a table just as a huge spotlight hit the stage, revealing Tina Carlyle in a glittering gold dress. The Mask's eyes bugged out as he watched Tina sing a song about love and money. A loud horn sounded, and his heart shot out of his chest about two feet with each beat. Clouds of steam spurted out of his ears and the Mask shouted *"Yowza!"* Then he started whistling, banging his fists on the table, and stomping his feet.

Tina kept singing without missing a beat. When she finished, the audience stood up and cheered wildly. But the Mask was the wildest of all. He zipped around the club's dance floor, ending up on top of the piano.

He stared down at the black-suited piano player, who was frowning back up at him.

"Let's *rock* this joint!" the Mask yelled, and gave the pianist's stool a hard spin.

When the pianist came to a stop, he had been transformed into a leather-clad rocker who started banging out a fast-moving popular song.

The Mask liked the music, so he leapt onto the dance floor. He grabbed the astonished Tina and the two of them began dancing at warp speed. The crowd cleared a space for them, admiring the amazing moves the couple made. The Mask spun Tina around like a baton. Then he hit the floor himself in a series of splits.

"S-s-smokin'!" he shouted, and the onlookers burst into noisy applause.

The Mask was just getting started.

On the dance floor it was party time, but upstairs in Dorian Tyrel's office, an unhappy meeting was just getting started. Dr. Freeze and the others had returned to report their disaster at the bank.

"Where's the money?" Dorian demanded.

Dr. Freeze shrugged. "Someone else hit the place before we did, man."

Dorian sank back in his chair, covering his face. This was bad news he *didn't* want. And Niko wasn't going to like it either. "Who?" he asked.

"Don't know," Dr. Freeze said. "Dude looked like some kind of geek-monster. Next thing we know, the cops show up."

Sweet Eddy suddenly did a double take at the TV monitor that showed what was happening in the club downstairs. On the screen, the Mask was dancing like a maniac with Tina.

"That's him!" he said. "That's the guy!"

Dorian's mouth fell open. "He takes our money

and then walks right into *my* club?" He grabbed a gun from his desk and headed for the door. "Come on! This guy is *history!*"

The problem with Stanley is he's just too nice. His friend Charlie tells him, "Nice guys finish last."

Stanley puts the ancient mask on and checks himself out in the mirror. "S-s-snazzy!" he shouts.

"Can't make the scene without the green," cries the Mask, carrying huge sacks of money out of the bank.

The Mask's eyes bug out as he watches Tina, the girl of his dreams, sing at the CoCo Bongo Club.

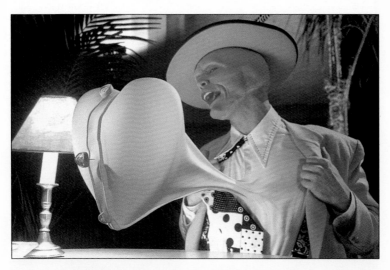

The Mask's heart shoots out of his chest with each beat of Tina's song.

"Let's rock this joint!" the Mask cries out, swaying to the music.

The Mask's dream comes true–a dance with Tina!

"You got me, pardner!" gasps the Mask, morphing into a cowboy.

"I got the beat!" the Mask sings out as he dances in the street.

Stanley tries to convince a psychiatrist of the mask's special powers.

When bad guy Dorian puts the mask on, his evil eyes glow with wicked power.

"You missed me! You missed me!" sings the Mask as the crooks close in on him. "Now you gotta kiss me!"

Stanley and Tina toss the mask into the swirling river. But there's no way of knowing when—or where—it will pop up next!

CHAPTER EIGHT

On the dance floor, the Mask was spinning Tina around and around like a top. She moved so fast that real smoke rose up from her heels as they whipped around the polished wood of the dance floor.

"Clear the club!" Dorian yelled as he tore down the stairs. "Now!"

Bobby the bouncer jumped to obey.

In seconds, the place was almost empty except for Tina and the Mask, who were still spinning away. Now the Mask jerked Tina to a halt, bent her over backward, and planted an exaggerated kiss on her lips.

Tina lost her balance and grabbed at the Mask's tie for support—just as a gun was fired. The bullet shot the tie in half. Tina fell to the floor, as did the piece of tie, which morphed back into a piece of Stanley's purple paisley pajamas.

Dorian aimed his still-smoking gun at the Mask. "All right, twinkle-toes. I want to know where my money is, and I want to know now."

Immediately, the Mask whipped out an old-fashioned metal cash register and started counting. Each time he pressed a button, the machine gave a ringing *Ka-ching!*

"I'll tell you where your money is," the Mask said, fast-talking. "You've got 17.5 percent in T-bills amortized over the fiscal year and 8.75 percent in stocks and bonds." He pressed buttons with *Ka-ching* after *Ka-ching*. "Carry the nine and divide by the gross national product, and—"

"Cut that out!" Dorian shouted, and nudged Sweet Eddy. "Ice him."

Eddy started shooting his gun.

Blam! Blam! Blam!

The Mask dodged each bullet easily with his cartoon-flexible body. *Blam!* He spun into the shape of a bullfighter, waving his red cape in front of Eddy and Dorian.

"Get him!" roared Dorian. But they couldn't because the Mask kept changing shapes and leaping over bullets.

Finally, the Mask spun into a cowboy. This time he took the hits and staggered backward. "You got me, pardner," he gasped, throwing an arm around Sweet Eddy for support. "Tell Auntie Em to let Old Yeller out." He gasped and choked out names of characters in famous films. "Tell Tiny Tim I won't be home for Christmas, I—I—" The Mask's pink tongue flopped out of his mouth as he collapsed onto the dance floor.

Eddy burst into tears as he stared down at the Mask.

A large cartoon audience suddenly appeared, applauding and cheering his performance. An Oscar was handed to the Mask.

Instantly, the Mask sprang to his feet, taking bows. Now he was wearing a gaudy purple and orange ball gown and seemed close to tears.

"Thank you!" he cried. "You love me! You *really* love me! And if we could all just send good thoughts to Tibet—"

"*I* don't love you!" Dorian roared, and started shooting again.

In a flash the Mask was back in his suit and zipping out one of the club's windows. A second later, the nightclub doors were kicked open. "Get that geek!" Dorian shouted.

But it wasn't the Mask returning—it was the police!

"Freeze!" Lieutenant Kellaway yelled.

Dorian let his arm drop, the gun clattering to the floor. "Got a legal right to search this place, Kellaway? Or did you just drop by thinking you'd get a free soda?" he sneered.

"You bet I'm here legally," Lieutenant Kellaway said. "Some of your people were spotted trying to rob the bank." He frowned. "And *one* of them was wearing a big green mask and a purple paisley suit."

"He's not one of *my* guys," Dorian said sulkily.

"Search the place, boys," Lieutenant Kellaway ordered before snapping handcuffs onto Dorian's wrists. "In the meantime, you and I are going downtown for a little chat."

On their way out, Lieutenant Kellaway noticed some fabric on the floor—it had once been the Mask's tie. He picked it up and studied the purple paisley design. It matched the description of one of the bank robber's outfits. *And* the pattern was also a perfect match to Stanley Ipkiss's unique pajamas.

Now Lieutenant Kellaway knew exactly where he was going next—and who he was going to arrest when he got there.

A few hours later, Stanley was awakened by a loud pounding on his front door. The noise made his head ache even more than it already did. But he slowly struggled out of bed and stumbled toward the door. Then he spotted the mask on his dresser. He knew he had to hide it—quickly! He grabbed the mask, opened the closet door—and a mountain of cash poured out, almost smothering him.

"Police, open up!" Lieutenant Kellaway yelled. "I know you're in there, Ipkiss!"

For a moment, Stanley stared at the piles of cash at his feet. *Where had it all come from?* he wondered. Then the pounding on the door started again. There was no time to figure it out. He had to get rid of the bills fast! Using Milo's Frisbee, Stanley frantically shoveled the money back inside the closet. The pounding on the door got louder.

"I'll be right there!" he called. He kicked a few stray bills under the bed, slammed the closet shut, and then went to open the front door. "You're up bright and early this morning, Lieutenant," he said pleasantly. "Won't you come in?"

But Lieutenant Kellaway had already come in. "Where were you earlier this evening, Ipkiss?" he demanded.

"Uh, here," Stanley said. "Mostly. Is something wrong?"

"What do you know about this 'Mask' character?" Lieutenant Kellaway asked. "And don't try to con me, because I found *this* at the CoCo Bongo." He held out the torn piece of fabric, which exactly matched the piece missing from Stanley's pajamas. "And the Mask character was wearing an outfit that looked like *your* pajamas when he robbed the Edge City Bank, where *you* work."

Milo, who was yapping by the closet door, leapt up, trying to open it.

"Milo, no!" Stanley said, and pushed him away.

"May I see the pajamas you were wearing yesterday morning?" Lieutenant Kellaway asked.

"They were stolen," Stanley said immediately.

"They were stolen," the lieutenant repeated.

"You heard me," Stanley said, batting Milo back from the door again. "I mean, what's this city coming to when a man's pajama drawer is no longer safe? What do we pay you people for anyway?"

Lieutenant Kellaway's eyes narrowed. He had no choice but to go. The evidence wasn't strong enough to arrest Stanley.

"All right, but don't even think of leaving town," he said, scowling at Stanley and Milo. "I'll be in touch."

Lieutenant Kellaway slammed the front door just as the closet door fell open, spilling all the cash. Happily, Milo snatched his Frisbee and went off to play with it.

"What are we going to do, Milo?" Stanley asked. He kicked at some of the cash.

His life was much more exciting now that he'd found the mask. But there was a definite possibility that he was going to get caught soon. Then he'd be locked up for life.

Stanley fell back on his bed. How would he ever get away with this?

CHAPTER NINE

At the police station, Lieutenant Kellaway and some of the other officers were studying the grainy videotape taken from the security camera at the bank. A blurred image of the Mask was visible as he zigzagged around the vault at top speed. There was a wild-eyed look of glee on his face as he stuffed sacks full of money.

"That is some mask," Officer Doyle remarked.

"Get the bank employee files and run down the fingerprints on a guy named Stanley Ipkiss," Lieutenant Kellaway said.

"You figure the robbery was an inside job?" Doyle asked.

"All we need is for Ipkiss's fingerprints to match the ones we found all over the bank vault," Lieutenant Kellaway said. He frowned. "And then I'm going to lock that wacko up until doomsday."

At the CoCo Bongo Club, Dorian had summoned a war council to his office. It included other members of the city's criminal gangs. He held up a briefcase filled with bundles of money.

"I'll give fifty grand to the guy who finds that green-faced moron before the cops do," Dorian said. He punched his fist against the table. "I want him here! Alive! By tomorrow!"

The men took off, racing to see who would find him first.

Tina, who was sitting in the corner reading a newspaper's great review of her performance, glanced up. "You're losing it, Dorian," she said.

"All I know is that when this is over, there's going to be payback for anyone who's double-crossing me." He paused significantly and looked at Tina. "And I mean *anyone*."

"Hey, all I did was take pictures of the bank like you asked." Tina said. "And I won't be doing anything like that again. I'm a singer now, out of the crime business."

"Oh, yeah?" Dorian said with a cruel laugh. "Without me you're nothing."

"Don't push me," Tina shot back. "I just might take the walk I should have taken a long time ago."

"You try it, baby," Dorian said threateningly.

Tina shrugged and went back to the review. She was afraid of Dorian—but she was never going to let him know that.

Stanley limped into work late. His face was

pale, and dark circles ringed his eyes. The bank was still a mess, and worried customers were milling around everywhere.

"Ipkiss!" Mr. Dickey, the top bank officer, shouted. "We have a crisis here and you stroll in over an hour late! Who do you think you are?"

Stanley stopped, suddenly developing an odd facial twitch. "Back off, monkey boy!" he snarled. "Or I'll tell your daddy you're running this place like your own personal piggy bank."

Mr. Dickey was stunned into silence. "Uh, okay," he said, backing away. "No problem. You, uh, have a nice day, Ipkiss."

"What side of the bed did *you* fall out of?" Charlie asked Stanley when he got to his desk. He'd never heard Stanley say a mean word to anyone.

"I'm not sure," Stanley said, twitching slightly. "I haven't been myself lately." For a split second, his entire face took on an alarming Masklike grimace. "I'm—a little on edge."

"Well, I've got just what you need," Charlie said. "Two tickets to the charity ball at the CoCo Bongo Saturday night. Want to go?"

"I don't know, Charlie, I—" Stanley stopped as he spotted Tina on her way in. He quickly walked over to meet her. "What are you doing here, Tina?"

"I heard about the robbery," she said. "I wanted to make sure you were okay."

65

Stanley grinned shyly. "I'm fine," he said. "I mean, really great. Here, sit down. I've been thinking about your account, and I think I can arrange a very good—"

Tina held her hand up to stop him. "Stanley, wait," she said. "I don't think I'll have much money to open a bank account with anymore."

"What about the singing?" he asked. "I thought you were doing great."

Tina sighed and folded her hands unhappily in her lap.

"What is it?" he asked.

"It's not your problem," she said, sounding miserable. "I'm just not sure how much longer I can stay at the CoCo Bongo."

"Well—maybe you could get a record deal," Stanley said.

Tina shook her head. "It's not that easy. There are thousands of singers out there just like me who—"

"*Not* just like you," Stanley said. "You've got a voice like an angel—er, so the newspaper reviews say." Just in time he realized that he *as himself* hadn't actually heard Tina sing—the Mask had.

Tina sighed. "That's sweet, Stanley, it really is. But you have to have connections with people in the music business to make it. Nobody can make it out there on their own. *Nobody*." She sighed again. "Well, anyway. I'm just glad you're okay."

"You didn't stop by here just to see me, did

you?" Stanley asked curiously.

Tina hesitated. "Well—the guy they say robbed this place..."

Stanley nodded. "The Mask."

"I think he was at the club last night," Tina said.

"They, uh"—Stanley didn't quite meet her eyes—"say he's pretty weird-looking."

"Yes, but you should see him dance," Tina said dreamily. Then she recovered herself. "Well, I guess I'd better get going."

"You'd like to see him again, wouldn't you?" Stanley asked.

Tina nodded. "I—wouldn't mind."

"I know him," Stanley said boldly.

Now Tina looked impressed. "You do?"

"Yep," Stanley said. "We're, um, old college buddies. Funny you should mention his dancing." He made a little move with his feet. "I taught him everything he knows."

"Could you have him meet me tomorrow night?" Tina asked eagerly. "At Landfill Park? I won't turn him in."

"I...might be able to arrange that," Stanley said. "Like, around sunset?"

Tina beamed at him. "That's perfect," she said. "Thanks, Stanley. You are such a nice guy."

"Yeah," Stanley said, his shoulders sagging. "That's what they tell me."

* * * * *

Peggy Brandt, the reporter for the *Evening Star*, was just getting home after a long night. As she locked her car, she noticed a shadowy figure watching her from a dark corner of the parking garage. She clutched her purse to her side, hurrying down the row of parked cars.

The figure followed.

"Psst!" he said with a voice that sounded as if he'd been gargling glass. "I heard you need a newspaper story."

"Wh-who are you?" she asked shakily.

"Just a guy with some information looking to see some justice done," the stranger said. He was still standing in the shadows, so Peggy couldn't see his face.

The guy sounded like he was telling the truth. If there was a story here, and if the newspaper printed it, Peggy could get promoted to reporter. And that paid a lot more money than the "Ask Peggy" column. "Maybe we can work something out," she said. "What's this about?"

"It's about the Mask and why Dorian Tyrel's willing to pay fifty large ones to get him." With that, the mysterious figure told Peggy the whole tale.

"So how do I find this Tyrel guy?" Peggy asked.

"Careful, careful," the figure whispered, before melting into the darkness. "You break this story, and he just might find *you*."

Peggy was more than willing to take that chance.

CHAPTER TEN

Bright and early the next day, two of Niko's tough guys "escorted" Dorian to a meeting with their boss. Niko, who was playing golf on his high-tech indoor range, looked up when the thugs dumped Dorian on the floor.

"Thanks for dropping by, Dorian," he said.

Dorian grumbled and got up, brushing himself off.

"Golf is an interesting game," Niko remarked, taking a solid swing. "It takes concentration. Focus. If your mind wanders, you lose. And you know how much I hate to lose."

Dorian hung his head.

"The cops tell me they're going to shut my CoCo Bongo Club down," Niko said. "I hear things like that—and my golf game goes right down the tubes." He frowned at Dorian. "I'm going to give you a break, though. You have a week to get out of town. If you're not gone..." Niko demonstrated with a vicious swing of his

70

golf club what would happen to Dorian. "Is that clear?"

Dorian nodded grimly. "Crystal," he said.

That morning, when Stanley went out, he found a picture of himself—as the Mask, in the grainy bank video—on the front page of the town's newspaper. The reporter credited with breaking the story was Peggy Brandt.

Looking paler and more desperate than ever, Stanley continued walking down the street toward work. Then, in a store window, he caught sight of a book called *The Masks We Wear* by Dr. Arthur Neuman, the psychiatrist he had seen on the Larry King show. Maybe this man could help him. After all, Dr. Neuman had written a whole book about masks. Stanley felt in his pockets for some change and went to call for an emergency appointment.

He was given one for late that afternoon. He brought the mask along with him to the office for Dr. Neuman to see.

"Very interesting," Dr. Neuman said, examining the mysterious carvings in the wood. "Could be one of the Viking night gods. Maybe Loki, the god of mischief." He put the mask down and gave Stanley a too-sweet smile. "Loki caused so much trouble, they say, he was locked away forever."

Stanley gasped. "You mean he was turned into a mask?"

Dr. Neuman chuckled at that idea. "Mr. Ipkiss,

that's just an ancient story. This mask is nothing but a piece of wood."

"But what about your book?" Stanley asked, confused.

"My book isn't about *real* masks. It's about the way we change ourselves so other people will like us," Dr. Neuman explained. He chuckled again. "I think you're just suffering from a mild delusion, Mr. Ipkiss."

"I'm telling you," Stanley insisted, "when I put this thing on, I become a completely different person. The mask has a life of its own!"

"Really," Dr. Neuman said, sounding bored. "And does it talk to you?"

"Well—right before I put it on," Stanley admitted. "It, uh, kind of whispers my name."

"The mask doesn't know your name," Dr. Neuman said. "But *you* know your name." He pursed his lips. "Does the mask ever say things to you your mother used to say? Hmmm?"

"I'm not having delusions," Stanley said quietly.

"Mr. Ipkiss, I have people sitting in my waiting room right now who deserve to see me," Dr. Neuman said. "You, on the other hand, only *think* you do. That is a delusion."

"All right," Stanley said, and took a deep breath. "I'll prove it to you." Slowly, he placed the mask on his face and began to spin. But something was wrong. He wasn't picking up speed. He wasn't whirling around like a tornado.

Stanley kept spinning and spinning. Nothing happened. He tried again and again, and still absolutely nothing happened. He frowned and lowered the now apparently harmless mask.

"Mr. Ipkiss, I do have other patients to see today," Dr. Neuman said after an awkward pause.

"Wait! You said that the Viking god Loki was a night god. Maybe the mask works only at night," Stanley said uncertainly.

But Dr. Neuman was no longer listening. He stood up and handed Stanley a copy of his book. "Here. It's on the house. Good luck."

Stanley headed for the door. It was obvious that he was on his own.

Outside, Lieutenant Kellaway and Officer Doyle were parked in an unmarked police car. They had been trailing Stanley for hours. As they waited for him to come out of the doctor's office, the radio crackled.

"I've got the cross-check from the bank files, Lieutenant," one of the officers at headquarters said. "Those fingerprints on the bank vault are Stanley Ipkiss's. You want us to pick him up?"

Lieutenant Kellaway smiled as Stanley came outside and hailed a taxi.

"Just keep the SWAT team standing by," he said. "If this guy's half as bad as I think, we're going to need all the help we can get." Then he elbowed Officer Doyle. "Follow that car!"

The officer nodded and started the engine.

They were not going to let Stanley out of their sight.

A few minutes later, Stanley directed the cab to let him off at Landfill Park to meet Tina. When she saw him, she stood up from the park bench where she had been waiting, looking very surprised.

"What are *you* doing here, Stanley?" she asked.

"I—just wanted to make sure you two got together okay," Stanley said lamely.

"That's nice," Tina said, and sat back down. "You know, I hardly ever come out here. I forgot how pretty it is."

Stanley nodded. "Especially at sunset. The exhaust clouds from the factories really pick up the colors."

"Wow, they sure do," Tina said, following his gaze. "How lovely."

They both sat and admired the view.

"You know, I was thinking about what you said and maybe you're right," Tina said finally. "I *am* a good singer. And if I believed in myself more, maybe I wouldn't rely on guys like Dorian."

Stanley stared at her. "You mean Dorian Tyrel?"

Tina nodded. "He's sort of my manager," she said.

Stanley looked worried. "Tina, you have to be careful of that guy," he said. "He's trouble. He's a very dangerous criminal!"

"Look, I can take care of myself," Tina said defensively. "I always have. Besides, Dorian's the one who gave me the job at the CoCo Bongo."

"If you really had any faith in yourself, you wouldn't be hanging on to someone else for a free ride," Stanley said.

A dark shadow fell over them as the last rays of sun disappeared behind the clouds. Realizing that he had hurt Tina's feelings, Stanley got up.

"I'm sorry, Tina," he said. "I do everything wrong. I—I'd better get going."

"Stanley, wait!" she called.

But he was already gone.

CHAPTER ELEVEN

Tina started to follow him, but a fierce wind blew her back. With a strange *Whoosh!* the leaves around her kicked up, and the Mask suddenly leapt out of the trees in all of his purple-suited glory.

"Ma chere! Je t'aime!" he shouted in French, telling Tina he loved her. Then he swept her off her feet with a big smile. "At last we are together, *mon petit bonbon!"*

Tina smiled back at him, but she couldn't help wondering where Stanley was.

On the other side of town, in the newsroom at the *Evening Star*, a veteran reporter named Murray ran in and grabbed his coat.

"Looks like it's going to be a long night," he said to Peggy. "The cops have your pal Ipkiss staked out at Landfill Park. We just heard it over the police radio."

Peggy jumped to her feet. "Let me cover it,

Murray! Please! I need this story!"

Murray hesitated. "I'm not sure, Peggy. Maybe—"

"Thanks a million," Peggy said. Before he could say no, she grabbed her sweater and ran out of the room.

Back at Landfill Park, the Mask was trying to charm Tina, who was looking more frightened by the second.

"Our love is like a red, red rose," he said. His heart popped out from his chest and took on the shape of a pulsing red rose.

Tina edged farther away from him.

The Mask grabbed the rose and pushed it back inside his suit. "And now for the real thing—" He threw his arms wide and lunged for Tina, who ducked out of the way.

"Freeze!" Lieutenant Kellaway yelled, jumping out of the bushes.

The Mask froze in midair, his arms outstretched and his feet suspended off the ground.

"Put your hands up!" Lieutenant Kellaway ordered.

"But you told me to freeze, so how can I move?" the Mask said, his lips hardly even twitching.

"All right, all right, unfreeze," Lieutenant Kellaway said impatiently. "You're under arrest!"

The Mask crashed to the ground and began writhing wildly about. "Under arrest? No!" he cried out. "It wasn't me! It wasn't me!"

As the police moved in on him, he suddenly stopped moving and put his head in his hands. "Oh, what's the use? I confess. I was so young! So foolish! So full of life!" He looked at Lieutenant Kellaway maniacally, tears gushing out of his eyes like twin faucets.

Lieutenant Kellaway wasn't sure what to say, so he just snapped the handcuffs around the Mask's rubbery wrists. "Search him," he said to Officer Doyle.

Doyle started going through the Mask's pockets and throwing things on the ground. "Comb, Flintstones vitamins, tuba, slingshot..." he said as he tossed each object down.

The police stared at the growing mountain of stuff at the Mask's feet. The Mask took advantage of their shock and drew a sword from his hidden pocket. With three quick strokes, he cut a *Z* in Lieutenant Kellaway's shirt.

"Adios, amigos!" he yelled, and ran off.

Lieutenant Kellaway started after him, but discovered that he was now handcuffed to Doyle. Once again, the Mask had outwitted him.

"After him!" he ordered into his police radio.

The Mask zoomed outside the twelve-foot-high stone wall surrounding the park. He slammed the immense wooden gates behind him. He threw an iron bolt. Then he snapped on a huge padlock and smashed down a steel plate. He zipped up a gigantic zipper, hammered in dozens of nails, and then threw himself against the gate.

"Whew!" he said, and wiped an oversize hanky across his forehead. But then his eyes bugged out on stalks when he saw that he was surrounded by cops outside the park.

There were cops in cars, cops in armored trucks, cops hanging from trees, and cops parachuting from helicopters. And they were all aiming big guns at him.

The Mask looked around, trying to figure a way out, and snapped his fingers.

"Hit it!" he yelled.

With that, a police spotlight came on and the park entryway turned into a beautifully lit stage. The Mask bowed and became a performer with a ruffled light blue shirt. Passersby with radios and big boom boxes looked down in shock as a loud, fast Spanish dance called the rumba began playing from every speaker in town.

The Mask began singing in a heavy Spanish accent and dancing at lightning-quick speed. He winked and nodded to the crowd. He performed high-flying flips and splits. This was his big number, and he was going to enjoy every second!

"Yessir, I've got the beat!" the Mask sang. "I'm the craze of my native street!"

"You know," Officer Doyle said from the top of the wall where he and Lieutenant Kellaway were watching, "he's not half bad."

Lieutenant Kellaway gave him a dirty look.

The Mask waved his arms and coaxed the cops into joining in. Like a rough-and-tumble group of dancers, they began to step in time to the infectious beat.

Lieutenant Kellaway was so shocked, he fell right off the wall. His cops, his tactical squad, his SWAT team—they were all in the street, dancing with this masked lunatic!

"You idiots!" he shouted. "Arrest that thing!"

Suddenly ashamed of themselves, the cops stopped dancing and fumbled for their weapons.

In the meantime, the Mask took off, dashing into the crowd. Realizing how easy he was to spot, he pulled at his head.

The Mask stretched like taffy, and let out a high-pitched wail. Then it was transformed back into a piece of wood.

Stanley was himself again.

He slipped the mask under his jacket and tried to blend in with everyone else, but Lieutenant Kellaway had already seen him.

"Halt!" the police officer yelled. "Halt, or we'll shoot!"

Stanley looked around and saw that cops were closing in from every direction. He was trapped!

CHAPTER TWELVE

Quickly, Stanley cut down a narrow alley with the cops hot on his trail. Just as he reached the next street, a car squealed to a halt next to him.

"Stanley!" Peggy Brandt yelled from the open window. "Get in!"

Stanley didn't argue. He dove through the window into the passenger seat. Peggy stepped on the gas and the car screeched off.

"Where are we going?" he asked.

"Someplace we'll be safe!" Peggy told him.

They ended up in the shadowy shipping room at the newspaper building. They sat down on stacks of bound newspapers, watching as the printing press beyond them spewed out the following morning's edition.

"I saw the whole thing," Peggy said, handing him a cup of coffee. "What's with you, Stanley?"

Stanley shook his head. "I don't know," he said. "It's crazy. When I put on this mask, I can do anything—but it's ruining my life."

"Whatever this mask is, you don't need it," Peggy said. "That letter you sent to my column was full of more heart and guts than any guy I know. You're already all you ever need to be."

"Gosh, Peggy," Stanley said, blushing. "Do you really mean that?"

She paused. "Actually, no."

Before Stanley could figure out what she meant by that, the door behind them burst open. He turned and saw Dorian and three of his men in the doorway. They were all holding guns.

Peggy stood up and spoke to Dorian. "I want to see the fifty thousand you promised before I tell you who the Mask is."

Sweet Eddy flicked open a briefcase full of cash.

"Good," Peggy said. "This Ipkiss guy is the one you've been looking for. When he puts on that wooden mask, he becomes that green thingama-jig."

Stanley stared at her, dumbfounded. "Peggy, what are you doing?"

She shrugged. "Sorry," she said. "You're a nice guy, but I need the money."

Sweet Eddy and one of the other thugs grabbed Stanley. They held him above the steel jaws of the whirring news press.

"Okay, Ipkiss," Dorian said. "Where's the money from the bank?"

When Stanley didn't answer immediately, they

moved him closer to the printing press.

"My apartment," Stanley said, frantic with fear. "It's in my apartment!"

"Thanks," Dorian with a smile. "Now, I believe you have a *pressing* engagement." The thugs were prepared to drop Stanley into the jaws of the press.

"Hey!" Peggy protested. "You said you wouldn't hurt him!"

"Okay," Dorian said. "One thing at a time." He toyed with the wooden mask. "How does this thing work, Ipkiss?"

"I don't know," Stanley said, struggling to get free. "You just put it on."

Dorian raised the mask to his face. With a crack of thunder, a hurricane of light and power swirled around him. But unlike Stanley's transformation, Dorian's was evil. When the light died away, the Dorian version of the Mask rose from a circle of black smoke. While Stanley had been a purple-suited mischief-maker in hyperdrive, Dorian was more like a hulking evil genie. His diamond earring was still visible, but his huge grin stretched out like a Tyrannosaurus rex's under green eyes that glowed with wicked power.

"Whoa," the Dorian Mask said, his voice a deep inhuman rumble. "What a *rush*."

"You okay, boss?" Sweet Eddy asked uneasily.

"Better than ever!" the Dorian Mask rumbled.

"Well." Peggy reached for the briefcase. "I

guess I'll be going home now."

The Dorian Mask sidled up to her threateningly. "*Must* you?" he asked. "What a shame. We could make...beautiful headlines together!"

"Forget it," Peggy said, backing out the door. "I wasn't born yesterday."

"I'll take care of you later," he shouted after her.

"Hey, boss, what do we do with Ipkiss?" Sweet Eddy asked nervously.

The Dorian Mask shrugged. "The police are looking for the Mask, so we'll give them the Mask." He put on a horrible smile. "Then we'll lay low until tomorrow night, when we pay a little visit to Niko's charity ball!"

They tied Stanley up, forced him into a car, and drove to his apartment. Then Dorian's henchmen went upstairs to get the money from Stanley's closet. Milo growled low and hid behind the curtains, where they wouldn't see him. Once they were gone, he peeked out the window and saw Stanley in the backseat.

Immediately, Milo ran downstairs and started chasing the car, dodging the traffic. Stanley was in trouble, and Milo was going to save him!

Lieutenant Kellaway and Officer Doyle were just getting back to the police station from Landfill Park.

"I can't believe it." Lieutenant Kellaway shook

his head as he walked up the front steps. "Hardened cops dancing in the streets, being directed by a dangerous criminal—and all of it on the ten o'clock news!"

"The SWAT team got an offer to perform on TV," Sergeant Doyle said, trying to cheer him up.

Lieutenant Kellaway ignored him. "The captain's going to have my badge for breakfast," he said glumly. "Unless, of course, Ipkiss falls right in my lap."

At that instant, a car sped by, its door flew open, and a body came tumbling out. The body sailed through the air and landed smack on top of Lieutenant Kellaway. Stanley, indeed, had fallen right into his lap!

"Don't worry," Stanley said before Lieutenant Kellaway could start yelling at him. "I can explain everything."

"Oh, yeah?" Lieutenant Kellaway yanked out a large green rubber mask that the thugs had stuffed in Stanley's pocket while he was tied up. The crooks knew it would get Stanley in trouble because it looked a lot like the green face of the Mask. "Then explain this!"

Stanley was speechless.

The next thing he knew, he was in jail.

His cell was small and dark. When he heard some yowling outside the tiny barred window, he climbed up on his battered cot to peer out.

Down in the street, Milo was barking wildly.

"You'd better forget about me and find a new owner, buddy," Stanley said sadly. "It looks like I'm going to be in here for a *long* time...."

Milo howled miserably—and Stanley felt like joining him.

CHAPTER THIRTEEN

Stanley spent the rest of the night lying on his cot, staring at the ceiling and feeling sorry for himself. The next morning, one of the muscle-bound guards appeared.

"Wake up," the man said gruffly. "You've got a visitor."

Stanley opened his eyes to see Tina standing on the other side of the bars.

"What are you doing here?" he said in surprise. "I mean—hi."

"Is it true?" she asked. "Are *you* the Mask?"

Stanley nodded sheepishly. "Yeah," he said. "But don't go blabbing it around. If I can get a smart lawyer, I can cut a deal with a judge and maybe get out of here soon."

Tina looked doubtful.

"Soon—like in a thousand years." Stanley slumped back down on his cot. "You'd better go. Your manager's going to get worried."

"I quit last night, Stanley," Tina said. "I just

came to tell you how sorry I am. About every-thing."

"You ran out on Dorian?" Stanley asked, hoping it was true.

Tina nodded. "That mask of yours turned him into a real monster," she said, and shuddered. "He's going to Niko's charity ball tonight and he's going to do something horrible."

"Like what?" Stanley asked. "Eat with his fingers?"

Tina stamped her foot. "Stanley, this is serious! There must be some way to stop him. How does the mask work?"

Stanley thought for a minute. "It brings your wishes to life—the good ones and the bad ones," he said slowly. "If, say, you wish you were more outgoing and romantic, you become this love-crazy wild man."

"And if you're like Dorian?" Tina asked.

The answer was almost too horrible to picture. "Then we're all in big trouble," Stanley said.

Tina nodded, wrapping her arms around herself. Then she said softly, "No matter what happens, thank you, Stanley."

"For what?" he asked.

"For believing in me when no one else did," she said. "For sharing a sunset with me. For being a romantic." Then she smiled. "I enjoyed our meeting in the park."

"That wasn't me," Stanley said. "That was—"

Tina shook her head. "No. Before. When you were you."

She moved closer to the bars. "When you were Stanley Ip—"

Their lips met briefly and sweetly through the bars.

"—kiss," she finished.

They smiled at each other.

"Time's up," the guard said roughly.

Tina sighed. "I have to disappear for a while, Stanley. So Dorian won't find me. I'm not sure where I'm going, but I'll let you know as soon as I can."

Stanley nodded, watching as the guard led her away. If their kiss had been a dream, he hoped he would never wake up.

Stanley stood on his cot to watch Tina through his window and was horrified to see Dorian's big limo waiting for her. Sweet Eddy jumped out and chased her up the alley.

"Hey!" Stanley shouted at the guard. "There's a woman being kidnapped out there! Do something!"

The guard ignored him and turned up the volume on his television show.

If anyone was going to help Tina, Stanley was going to have to do it alone! But how?

Outside, Tina ran down the street with Sweet Eddy close behind. Then Dorian's limo swerved in front of her, blocking her escape. The back door opened and Dorian stepped out, no longer wearing the mask. Even so, he still looked scary.

"Have a nice chat with the cops?" he asked Tina.

"I—I just wanted to see how much Ipkiss told them," she said, her voice shaking slightly.

"You two are getting awfully close, aren't you?" Dorian sneered. "Maybe it was *you* who helped him beat us to that bank job."

Tina shook her head angrily. "That's ridiculous, Dorian. I never—"

One of the other thugs, Orlando, interrupted. "Look what I found in her car, boss." He held up a small suitcase.

"Planning a little trip, angel?" Dorian asked in an evil tone.

"No, I—I—" Tina stuttered.

Dorian forced her into the limo. "Pick something pretty out of the travel bag for her to wear, boys," he said, pulling the mask out of his trench coat. "We're all going to crash a little party...."

Stanley paced around his cell, very upset. Then he got an idea. He climbed back on his cot and whistled for Milo.

"Here, boy!" he called. "Come on, boy!"

The little dog scrambled up from the spot where he been patiently waiting all night. Helplessly, he tried to reach the window. Then, finally, he began jumping on boxes and trash bags, using them as steps until he landed on top of a nearby Dumpster.

"Good boy," Stanley said. "Come on!"

Milo leapt up, but fell back into the trash.

"Come on, Milo!" Stanley urged.

Milo tried again. This time he made it all the way up to the window. Stanley shot out his arms, grabbed Milo, and pulled the little dog through the bars. They had a quick, happy reunion and then Stanley set him on the floor.

"Keys, Milo!" he whispered, pointing toward the guard. The man was fast asleep, a half-eaten ham and cheese sandwich in his lap next to the keys to the cell. "Get the keys!"

Milo trotted down the hall and returned a moment later.

"Good boy!" Stanley said. Then he frowned as he pulled a wedge of cheese out of the dog's mouth. "I said *keys,* not *cheese.* K-E-Y-S!"

This time Milo brought back the heavy key ring.

"Good boy!" Stanley said, unlocking the cell door. "Now let's go find Tina!"

They slipped out quietly, pausing to take the sleeping guard's gun on the way. Just as Stanley was sure they were home free, he and Milo bumped straight into Lieutenant Kellaway. Stanley panicked and pointed the gun at him.

"Don't be an idiot, Ipkiss," Lieutenant Kellaway said. "You're in the middle of a police station. There's no way you're going to just walk out of here."

"You're absolutely right," Stanley agreed. He grabbed Lieutenant Kellaway's gun with his free hand and shoved it in his pocket. Then he handcuffed the two of them together. "So I'm going to walk out of here *as your prisoner*."

Lieutenant Kellaway stared at him. "Are you crazy?"

"Just do it," Stanley said. He put on his toughest voice. "I'm a desperate man."

Tina was in trouble, and not even the entire Edge City Police Department was going to stop him from saving her!

CHAPTER FOURTEEN

In front of the CoCo Bongo Club, Dorian and Tina sat in his limousine. They were both dressed in fancy party clothes.

"It's almost time to crash Niko's charity ball," Dorian said, holding the mask on his lap. He winked at Tina and then flipped back a blanket on the seat beside him. Underneath were four small wooden crates marked DEMOLITION MATERIALS. "This is going to be a real *blast!*"

Then, as Tina watched in horror, Dorian raised the mask to his face to begin his transformation.

Inside the club, Niko was personally making sure that everything went smoothly. So far, over one hundred thousand dollars had been raised for charity and been stored in a giant plastic piggy bank above the dance floor. The whole place had been changed into a gambling casino. Guests in gowns and tuxedos were laughing and playing at poker tables and slot machines.

Everyone in town had come to enjoy the celebration, from the mayor to Stanley's friend Charlie, and even Mrs. Peenman! It was a night that they would never forget.

The party was in full swing when a loud *Kaboom!* exploded the front doors open. The security guards were knocked off their feet and blown inside, followed by Dorian, now the evil Mask. He stepped through the smoking ruins, dragging Tina with him. His gang was right behind them.

Niko stared at the bizarre-looking genie in the oversize suit. "Who are *you?*" he demanded.

"My, my, how quickly they forget," the Dorian Mask said mockingly. "I'm your favorite ex-employee, here to collect some payback." He showed his dinosaur teeth. "Give him a lesson on how to treat employees, boys."

Niko dove for cover as the gang began to tear the place apart. The crowd was thrown into a panic. Hordes of partygoers stampeded toward the exits, screaming in terror. Orlando fired a gun up at the plastic piggy bank and thousands and thousands of dollars began raining down on the floor. The rest of the gang began scooping up the money. They packed it into plastic garbage bags while Sweet Eddy sealed off the exits.

The Dorian Mask stood alone in the middle of the chaos with a wicked grin on his face. What a lovely time he was having at Niko's party!

Meanwhile, with Lieutenant Kellaway at his side, Stanley had had no trouble leaving the station house. Now the two of them and Milo were speeding in a police car to the CoCo Bongo Club.

"You're going to be locked up *forever*, Ipkiss," Lieutenant Kellaway predicted. He sat in the backseat with his hands cuffed behind him.

"Maybe," Stanley agreed, and turned on the siren.

When they got to the club, Stanley jammed on the brakes and looked over at Lieutenant Kellaway.

"I'm going to lock you in," Stanley said, waving the gun. "But use the radio and call for backup."

Lieutenant Kellaway looked confused. "You *are* nuts, aren't you?"

Stanley opened his door. "Trust me," he said. "We're going to need it!" He paused only long enough to pat Milo. "It's going to be dangerous in there, boy, so you stay."

He locked the doors and ran for the club entrance, but stopped short at the sight of Dorian's thugs in the doorway.

As Stanley frantically searched for a way to sneak in the back, the Dorian Mask tied Tina to the big palm tree in the middle of the waterfall's pool. His men were now wiring up the sticks of dynamite and setting a time clock.

"Don't do this!" Tina pleaded. "Let me go!"

"What's wrong, darling?" the Dorian Mask asked, laughing crazily. "Don't you want to go out with a *bang?*"

Just then Stanley found the kitchen entrance and was tiptoeing through it. When he peeked out through the doors, he saw a group of scared partygoers huddled together nearby. One of them was Charlie.

"Psst!" Stanley whispered. "Over here!"

Charlie turned around in surprise. "Stanley!" he said. "What are *you* doing here?"

Stanley motioned him over. "Start sneaking people out the back," he said.

Charlie shrugged, but he did as he was told.

Outside, Milo had managed to pop the car door lock and worm his way out of the car. Then he scurried toward the club as fast as his small legs could carry him.

In the meantime, Stanley was sneaking across the room to where Dorian's men were now frisking the partygoers for their cash and jewels.

Suddenly he was grabbed roughly by the collar.

"Hold it, Ipkiss!" Orlando said. "Hey, boss!" he shouted as he dragged his prisoner over to the waterfall. "Look who crashed the party!"

"How touching," the Dorian Mask said with a leer. "Just to show there's no hard feelings, I'm going to let you and Tina spend the rest of your lives together!"

"But it's *you* I love, Dorian," Tina said. "Please,

oh, please, can't I have one last kiss?"

The Dorian Mask hesitated and then shrugged. "Sure, why not?" He swaggered over to her.

Tina shook her head. "No! From the real Dorian." Her eyes looked dreamy. "Nobody's ever kissed me like Dorian Tyrel."

"This whole place is wired to blow anytime now," Sweet Eddy whispered urgently to his boss.

"Wait a minute," the Dorian Mask said, letting his pride get the best of him. "I'm going to give the girl one last thrill." He ripped the mask off and morphed back into his normal self. This was exactly what Tina had in mind. Her plan was working! With the mask in one hand, Dorian moved forward to kiss her.

Tina shot out a leg and drop-kicked the mask straight up into the air. It flew toward the ceiling in slow motion and then began tumbling back down.

Stanley, Dorian, and the thugs pushed and shoved at each other, all of them trying to get to the mask first.

It was a matter of life and death!

CHAPTER FIFTEEN

Out of nowhere, Milo sailed through the air and caught the mask as though it were a Frisbee. All those hours of playing Frisbee had finally paid off! Milo landed on the floor with the mask firmly in his mouth. But as he started to run away, one of Dorian's men grabbed his hind leg.

"Come here, you ugly little mutt," he grunted.

Milo pumped his legs frantically, but he was losing ground. At the last second he dropped the mask and jammed his muzzle into it. A deafening bark filled the club. Milo was transformed!

His pint-size doggy body now had an enormous green head with a double row of jagged canine teeth. His plain collar sparkled with diamond studs and his toenails were razor-sharp. He turned to look at Dorian's man, his eyes glowing with green fire.

"Whoa!" the man shouted, and quickly let go of the Milo Mask's leg.

In the midst of the confusion, Stanley rushed

over to Tina and started to untie her. Next to them, the bomb was ticking down.

"Stanley, hurry!" Tina urged, watching the second hand on the clock move. There were only sixty seconds to go before the bomb exploded!

"I am, I am!" Stanley said, but his fingers couldn't seem to loosen the knots.

Then Dorian spun Stanley around and slugged him in the face. As Stanley fell backward, he grabbed the crook's jacket. Both of them landed with a splash in the pool of water. They continued to fight, slipping and sliding and exchanging punches.

Over by the slot machine, Orlando was stalking the giant Milo Mask.

"Here, boy," he crooned. "Good doggie."

With one last flailing swing, Stanley nailed Dorian in the jaw. The thug went out like a light. Stanley looked down at what he had always thought of as a puny fist and smiled. Milo barked a deep victory *Woof!* and galloped over. The force of his leap knocked both of them down and Stanley got soaked all over again.

"Good boy, Milo," he said, and peeled off the mask.

With a dazzling *Shhwoop!* Milo was back to normal. But then the mask flew out of Stanley's hand. With *Zing!* and a *Ka-pow!* it sailed through the air and landed behind the bar.

Sweet Eddy and Orlando rushed over, but

Stanley was faster. He flung himself over the bar.

Immediately, the crooks started shooting at him. So much lead flew at the bar that nothing back there could possibly still be alive.

Then up popped Stanley—as the Mask!

"You missed me! You missed me!" he said in a singsong voice. "Now you gotta kiss me!"

Sweet Eddy and Orlando stared at the Mask, their mouths hanging open.

The Mask hopped over the bar and pulled a dozen guns from the pockets of his pinstriped suit. The huge gun barrels pointing out from the Mask's sides made him look like a human battleship.

"Do ya feel lucky, punks?" the Mask drawled, imitating a tough cop. "Well, do ya?"

Sweet Eddy and Orlando dropped their weapons and ran for the exit, shrieking every step of the way.

The bomb was still ticking down. Five, four, three, two—

"Stanley!" Tina screamed.

The Mask zipped over to Tina, grabbed the sticks of dynamite, and swallowed them all in one mighty gulp!

Tina stared up at him, her eyes shining bright.

"It was nothing," the Mask said modestly. "Nothing at all. Please."

Suddenly, there was an earthshaking explosion. For a split second the Mask's stomach swelled to gigantic proportions. His pupils spun like slot-machine numbers. Smoke came pouring out of his ears. Finally, his eyes clicked back into place and the Mask stood there with an odd but satisfied look on his face.

"Wow," he said, burping a great orange fireball. "That's some spicy meatball!" He burped out a little more fire and smoke. Then he finished untying Tina, who was still stuck on the palm tree island.

Behind him in the water, Dorian rose to his knees with a cruel glint in his eye. He reached under his jacket and pulled out a razor-sharp switchblade. Now he advanced toward the Mask and Tina.

The Mask sighed. "This guy does not know when to quit!" he said.

He began feeling along the trunk of the palm tree, searching for the lever that controlled the water in the falls and pool.

A few seconds later, he found a small glass panel hidden on the trunk of the tree. It read IN CASE OF EMERGENCY—BREAK GLASS.

The Mask smashed the glass with his pointy elbow. Magically, a large toilet-tank handle appeared. The Mask grinned as he pulled the metal lever down. As he yanked the handle, there was a loud *Swoooooosh!* and the entire pond flushed away. Dorian spun madly around and around in the center of the powerful whirlpool.

Then he was sucked down the pipes.

The Mask and Tina were left standing on the tiny palm tree island in the now-empty pond. The Mask pulled off his mask with a loud *Snap!* and became Stanley again.

"My hero!" Tina cried.

They both grinned, and hugged each other.

Down on the dance floor, Lieutenant Kellaway and a squad of police officers had just burst into the room, led by Charlie. Lieutenant Kellaway pointed at Dorian's henchmen and shouted, "Arrest those men!"

As the officers handcuffed the crooks, Lieutenant Kellaway headed to the palm tree. Stanley and Tina were still grinning at each another.

"It just kills me to interrupt you," Lieutenant Kellaway said. "But, Ipkiss, the party's over."

A heavyset man stepped in front of him. "Just a second, Officer."

"Look out, chunky," Lieutenant Kellaway snapped. Then he recognized the mayor of Edge City. "I mean, Mayor Tilton! I'm sorry, I didn't realize—"

Mayor Tilton scowled at him. "What's wrong with you?" he asked. "This young man just saved our lives!"

"With a little help from his friends," Charlie put in.

Lieutenant Kellaway looked around. "Where is

Dorian? He started all of this."

"Don't worry about him," Stanley said, and pointed to the empty pond. "All of his plans went right down the drain."

Lieutenant Kellaway looked from Stanley to the mayor. Then he sighed. "All right, Ipkiss," he said. "You're free to go. Just—don't hurry back, okay?"

Stanley grinned at him. Then he slung one arm around Tina and one around Charlie.

"Come on," he said. "We have one more stop to make before we call it a night."

The three of them drove in Charlie's car out to the deserted old bridge above the river. Milo sat in the back, wagging his tail and enjoying the ride.

Charlie parked the car in the center of the bridge, where Stanley had first seen the mask. "Are you sure you know what you're doing, buddy?" Charlie asked.

"I'm sure," Stanley said. He got out of the car, holding the mask very gently.

With Tina at his side, Stanley leaned over the bridge railing. He took a long last look at the mask's ancient wooden face.

"Are you sure you won't miss this guy?" he asked Tina. "If he's gone, all you're going to be left with is me."

Tina stared at him for a minute. Then she

smacked the mask out of his hands.

"I'll take that as a yes," he said with a grin.

The two of them watched as the mask plunged down, down, *down* into the swirling waters below. It went under the frothy waves, then bounced back up.

Stanley and Tina held hands but kept their eyes on the mask. They watched as it floated farther downstream. It began to move faster and faster, pulled along by the swift current.

And then, it was gone. Or was it? There was no way of knowing when—or where—the Mask would pop up next!